Fortunately, UNFORTUNATELY

First published in Great Britain in 2010 by Andersen Press Ltd.,

20 Vauxhall Bridge Road, London SW1V 2SA.

Published in Australia by Random House Australia Pty.,

Level 3, 100 Pacific Highway, North Sydney, NSW2060.

Copyright ©Michael Foreman, 2010.

The rights of Michael Foreman to be identified as the

author and illustrator of this work have been asserted by him

in accordance with the Copyright, Designs and Patents Act, 1988.

All rights reserved.

Colour separated in Switzerland by Photolitho AG, Zürich.

Printed and bound in Singapore by Tien Wah Press.

Michael Foreman has used watercolour paints in this book.

10   9   8   7   6   5   4   3   2   1

British Library Cataloguing in Publication Data available.

ISBN 978 1 84939 123 8 (Hardback)

ISBN 978 1 84939 224 2 (Paperback)

This book has been printed on acid-free paper

Fortunately, UNFORTUNATELY

MICHAEL FOREMAN

ANDERSEN PRESS

"Milo! Milo!"

It was Mum.

"Granny has left her umbrella here.
Can you take it round to her house, please?"

Fortunately,

it was a lovely day

and Milo liked going to Granny's house because she always had cakes for tea.

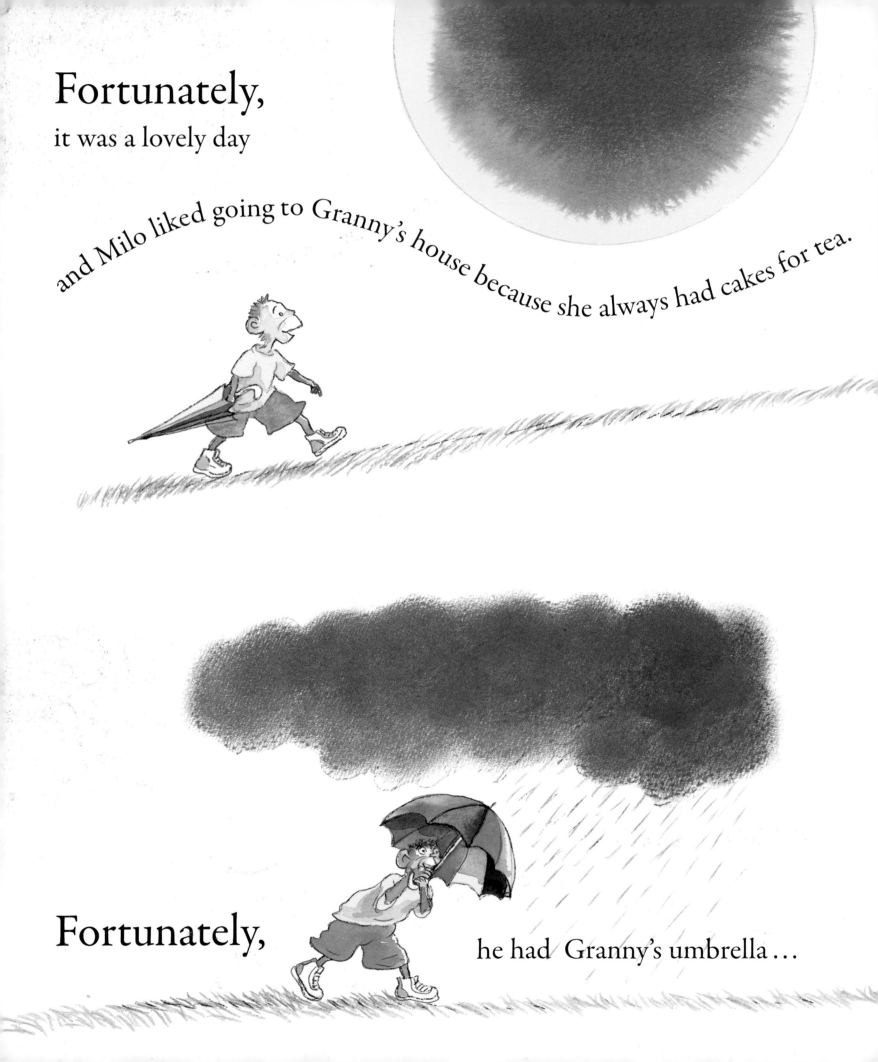

Fortunately,

he had Granny's umbrella …

Unfortunately,

a dark cloud appeared and it soon began to rain …

Unfortunately,

he didn't look where he was going …

Fortunately,

the umbrella was

like a parachute ...

Unfortunately, there was a whale...

Fortunately,
the umbrella kept Milo afloat inside the whale –
and there was a wonderful pirate ship …

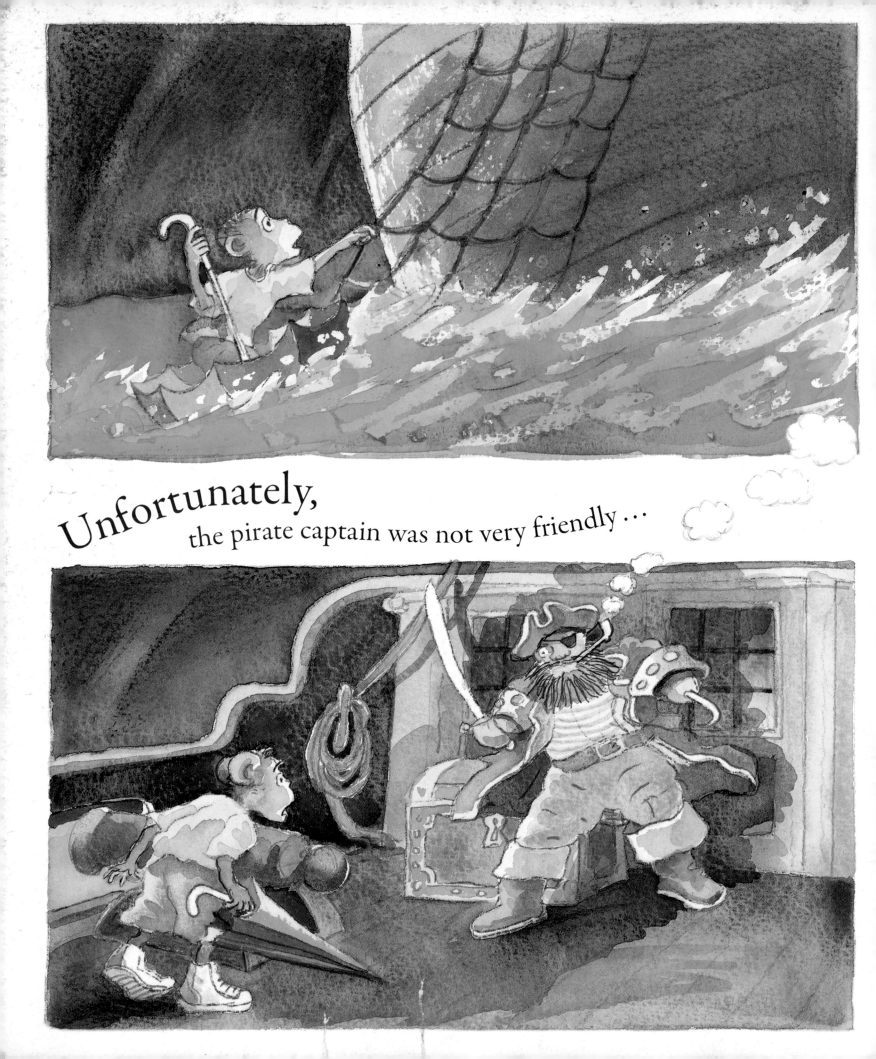

Unfortunately, the pirate captain was not very friendly ...

Fortunately,
he was not very good at sword fighting either …

Unfortunately, his pipe fell on the gunpowder...

Fortunately, Milo flew out of the whale's mouth...

Unfortunately, he was caught up in a TYPHOON...

...and dropped into a
Lost World at the top of
a volcano.

Fortunately, he splashed down in the blue waters of a lake . . .

Unfortunately,
it was full of wild dinosaurs ...

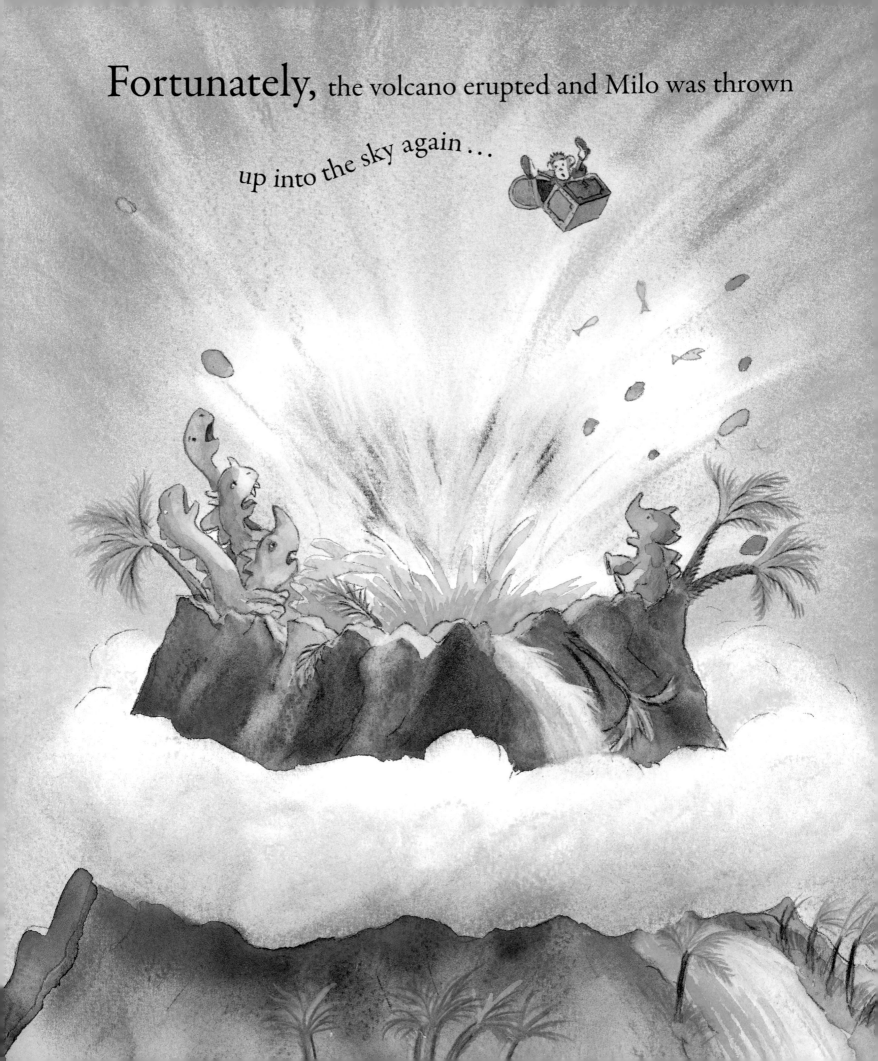

Fortunately, the volcano erupted and Milo was thrown

up into the sky again . . .

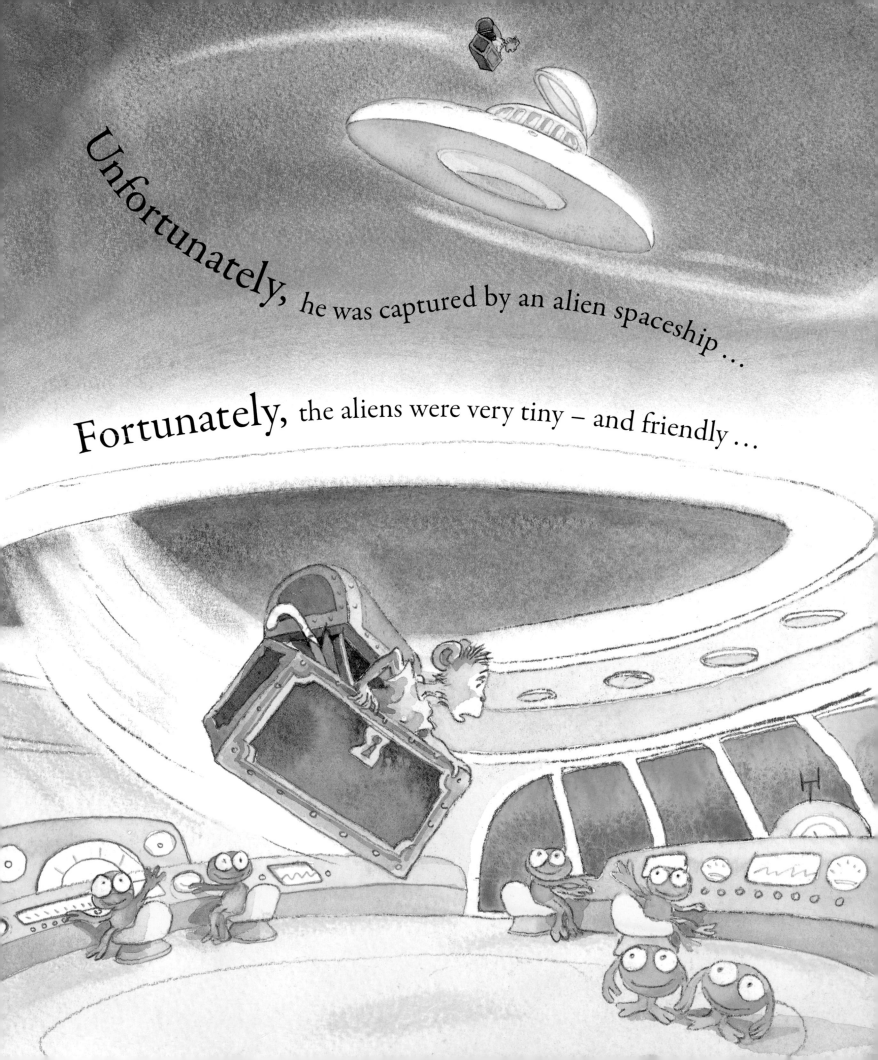

Unfortunately, he was captured by an alien spaceship …

Fortunately, the aliens were very tiny – and friendly …

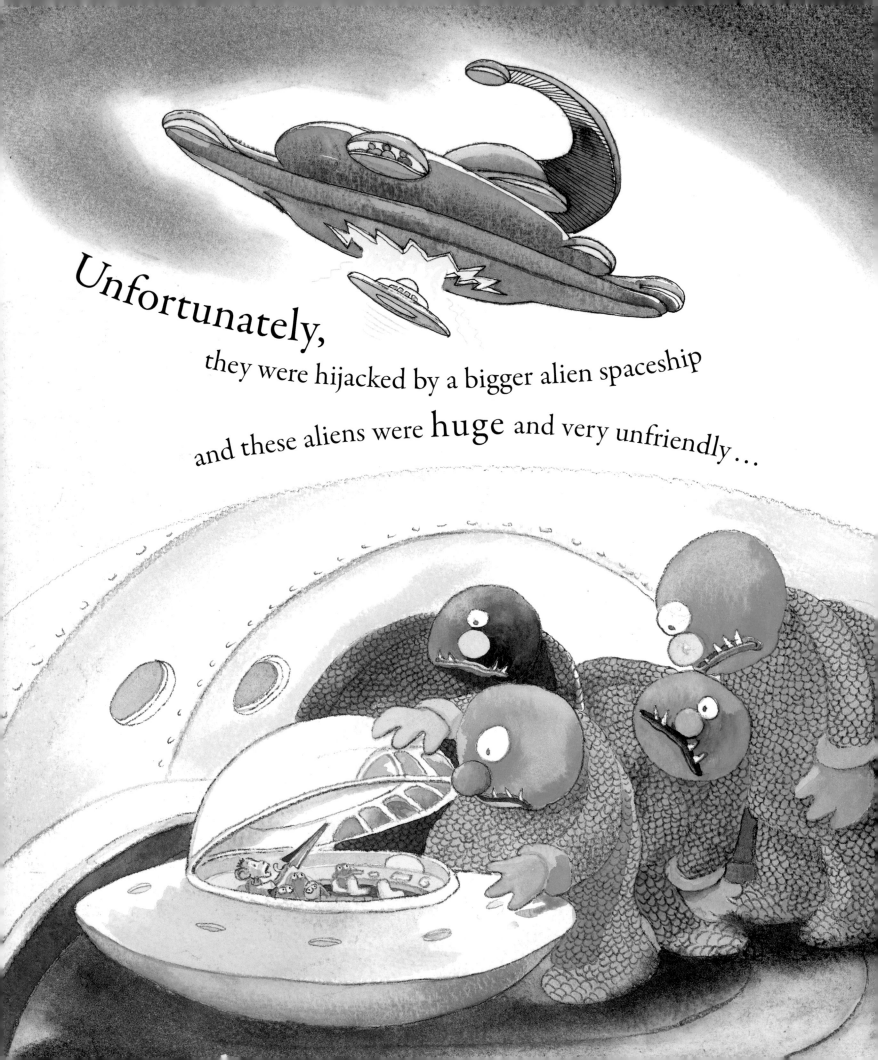

Unfortunately,
they were hijacked by a bigger alien spaceship

and these aliens were **huge** and very unfriendly . . .

Fortunately, they were just full of hot air and easily popped...
like **big** smelly balloons...

"Go! Go!" the huge aliens cried.

Fortunately, the little aliens flew Milo all the way to ...

Granny's house...

Unfortunately, Granny's umbrella was now a bit of a mess.

"What have you done to my umbrella?

Look at the state of it!"

Fortunately, it was full of pirate treasure . . .

Unfortunately, there was also a little alien . . .

Fortunately, his friends came back for him ...

And they all had tea . . .

Unfortunately . . .

"Come on, shipmates!
The old lady has got
our treasure . . ."

Other books by Michael Foreman:

THE LITTLE REINDEER

9781842705827

WONDER GOAL!

9781842709344

Norman's Ark

9781842705582

Seal Surfer

9781842705780

DINOSAUR TIME

9781849390477

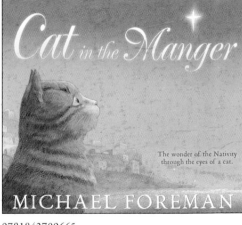

Cat in the Manger

9781842709665